Best Daddy
in all the World

GILL LOBEL &
VANESSA CABBAN

ORCHARD BOOKS

"Ha, ha, ha. Hee, hee, hee,
you can't catch me for a bumblebee!"
laughed Little Rabbit Short-Ears,
as he raced through the buttercups,
his white tail bobbing.

"Oh yes I can!" cried Daddy Rabbit.
And he caught Little Short-Ears between
his soft, strong paws.
"Now, little one," he said, "you can play
for a while – but remember, don't go out
of sight of our burrow . . ."

So Little Short-Ears waved goodbye to his daddy, and hopped off to play with his friends.

They played chase-my-tail round the old oak tree.
They leapt over the buttercups.
They played and played until Little Short-Ears
was hot and hungry. Then he saw it . . .

Far away, on the other side of the meadow, was a lovely patch of juicy pink clover!

With a flash of his tail, he was off.

Little Short-Ears forgot all about keeping his burrow in sight, as he bounced and nibbled, searching for the sweetest flowers – until he was far far away from his friends, and his home.

How tired he was! He yawned and
snuggled into a thick clump of ferns.
Bees droned in the buttercups,
and before long he was fast asleep.

Suddenly something wet hit Little Short-Ears
on the nose! He looked up at the sky.
Dark clouds scurried overhead.
Another drop of rain hit him on his head.
A cold wind whipped the grass. Icy raindrops
pinged his ears.

"I don't like it," he said. "I want my daddy!"
And he set off for his burrow . . .

Up the hill he bounded, then stopped.
He spun round, his heart thumping.
Everything looked wrong.
"This isn't my field!" he cried.
"Which way is home?"

Little Short-Ears ran and ran.

Then he heard the sound of his father's voice.

"Daddy," cried Little Short-Ears. "It's me!"

A big rabbit turned round.
"Who are you?" he said.
"I thought you were my daddy,"
gasped Little Short-Ears, "but you're not!"
He lifted up his face to the setting sun,
and cried and cried.

"Don't cry, little one," said Big Rabbit.
"I'll help you find your daddy."
Then he turned round and thumped
the earth with his mighty feet.

The hillside shook, and out of their burrows
the rabbits came tumbling!

"Tell us what your daddy is like," asked Big Rabbit.
Little Short-Ears struggled to get his breath.
"My daddy is the best daddy in all the world!" he sobbed.
"Tell us some more about your daddy," said a kind
mother rabbit.

"My daddy is the strongest daddy in all the world,"
said Little Short-Ears.

"Bigfoot is the strongest rabbit round here,"
cried one rabbit.

"What about Thunderpaws?" called another.

"Don't forget Big Bobtail!" said another.

"All you youngsters," said Big Rabbit, "go and find
the strongest rabbits, and bring them here!"
White tails flashed in the sunset.
Soon there was the sound of thunder on the hillside.

Three rabbits hurtled into sight.

Their chests were mighty.

Their legs were like tree trunks.

"Is one of these your daddy?" asked Big Rabbit.

Little Short-Ears looked at the faces in the
twilight, and rubbed a tear from his nose.

"No, none of these is my daddy," he said sadly.
"Tell us more about him," everyone asked kindly.
"My daddy has the longest ears in all the world!"
he whispered.

"Go and fetch Floppity," said Big Rabbit.
"And Willow, and Raindrop!"
Little Short-Ears waited anxiously.
Surely they would find his daddy now?

Over the hill flew swift feet. Six long silky ears gleamed in the silver light. Little Short-Ears gazed at the three smiling rabbits.

"No, none of these is my daddy," he sighed.

"Tell us more about him," said Kind Mother Rabbit,
patting him with her paw.
My daddy is the cuddliest daddy in all the world!"
he said.
"That's easy!" said all the rabbits. "Send for
Thistledown!"

Everyone watched as a big cuddly rabbit walked into
the circle. His smile was so friendly, and his silver fur so
soft and warm, that Little Short-Ears longed to stroke it.

But he shook his head with sorrow.
"No," he sniffed, "you are not my daddy.
"Perhaps I shall never see Daddy again!"
And a big tear rolled down his cheek.

Suddenly, there was the sound of scurrying feet,
and into the moonlit circle hurried a weary rabbit.
His tail was ragged, his ears were tattered, and some
of his whiskers were missing . . .

. . . but his eyes were shining with love.

Little Short-Ears leapt for joy, and hurled himself into his father's arms.

"There," Little Rabbit Short-Ears said proudly, "I told you my daddy was the best daddy in all the world!"